STEVENSON • WATTERS • ALLEN • LA

LUMBERJANES™

OUT OF TIME

BOOM!
BOX™

BOOM! BOX™

LUMBERJANES Volume Four, July 2016. Published by BOOM! Box, a division of Boom Entertainment, Inc. Lumberjanes is ™ & © 2016 Shannon Watters, Grace Ellis, Noelle Stevenson & Brooke Allen. Originally published in single magazine form as LUMBERJANES No. 14-17. ™ & © 2015 Shannon Watters, Grace Ellis, Noelle Stevenson & Brooke Allen. All rights reserved. BOOM! Box™ and the BOOM! Box logo are trademarks of Boom Entertainment, Inc., registered in various countries and categories. All characters, events, and institutions depicted herein are fictional. Any similarity between any of the names, characters, persons, events, and/or institutions in this publication to actual names, characters, and persons, whether living or dead, events, and/or institutions is unintended and purely coincidental. BOOM! Box does not read or accept unsolicited submissions of ideas, stories, or artwork.

A catalog record of this book is available from OCLC and from the BOOM! Studios website, www.boom-studios.com, on the Librarians Page.

BOOM! Studios, 5670 Wilshire Boulevard, Suite 450, Los Angeles, CA 90036-5679. Printed in China. First Printing.

ISBN: 978-1-60886-860-5, eISBN: 978-1-61398-531-1

THIS LUMBERJANES FIELD MANUAL BELONGS TO:

NAME:_____

TROOP:_____

DATE INVESTED:_____

FIELD MANUAL TABLE OF CONTENTS

LUMBERJANES
FIELD MANUAL

For the Intermediate Program

Tenth Edition • April 1984

Prepared for the
**Miss Qiunzella Thiskwin
Penniquiqul Thistle Crumpet's**
CAMP FOR ~~GIRLS~~

"Friendship to the Max!"

A MESSAGE FROM THE LUMBERJANES HIGH COUNCIL

Close your eyes and think of the happiest moment of your life. Really think about the details of that moment, where you were, the smell of the air, or if there were people with you. It's this moment that you truly felt joy, that you felt like you were part of something bigger than yourself in just a breath of time. It's these moments that we strive for with our Lumberjanes camp. Imagine a world in which you were not only motivated to succeed in any aspect of life, had any path available in front of you, and could also choose the stones in which the path was made. Personally, my path would by have been made of flagstone.

This volume of the Lumberjanes guide is meant to help any who hold it, anybody can take the lessons that are explained here and bring them to fruition in their everyday life, and the not so everyday life. The biggest lesson that we can teach you today is that time is fluid. It runs between our fingers quickly but it can also stand still, as if frozen in a moment. Time will never be controlled but that doesn't mean that it won't work for you when need most.

As you get older, you'll look at the past and wonder about all the things that could have been. About all the things you should have done, or maybe even the things you would have avoided if you had the same knowledge that you do today. You will think about the friendships that you created when you were young and innocent of the ways of the world and how those friendships grew into something amazing, or maybe they grew apart. At our camp we hope that you will be able to create friendships that will last with you until the very end of time, that will triumph over any obstacle and only grow stronger. And if these friendships should wane, then we hope it's a natural process of growing older and wiser, for we are all very different in our own ways and sometimes that means we have to take different paths on this crazy life.

THE LUMBERJANES PLEDGE

I solemnly swear to do my best
Every day, and in all that I do,
To be brave and strong,
To be truthful and compassionate,
To be interesting and interested,
To pay attention and question
The world around me,
To think of others first,
To always help and protect my friends,
~~To respect nature, myself and faith in God,~~
And to make the world a better place
For Lumberjane scouts
And for everyone else.

THEN THERE'S A LINE ABOUT GOD, OR WHATEVER

OUT OF TIME

Written by
Noelle Stevenson
& Shannon Watters

Illustrated by
Brooke Allen

Colors by
Maarta Laiho

Letters by
Aubrey Aiese

Cover by
Noelle Stevenson

Badges and Design by
Scott Newman

Associate Editor
Whitney Leopard

Editor
Dafna Pleban

*Special thanks to **Kelsey Pate** for giving the Lumberjanes their name.*

Created by **Shannon Watters, Grace Ellis, Noelle Stevenson & Brooke Allen**

CHAPTER THIRTEEN

Lumberjanes "Out-of-Doors" Program Field

SNOW-GLOBE TROTTER BADGE

"There's snow stopping us now!"

Traveling the world is just one of the many enjoyments of life, and being a Lumberjane is, for a large part, about enjoyment. Every Lumberjane should leave camp with the basic understanding of survival when it comes to any form of travel. Whether it be a sleeping party with just a blanket and the stars for company or a grand excursion through the tallest mountains she is able to find. A Lumberjane encounters many problems through life, but she will survive and thrive through them all. One of the many goals of the Lumberjanes is to make sure every young lady leaves with the tools to succeed. And some of these tools are taught as the Lumberjanes earns her *Snow-Globe Trotter* badge.

Traveling is a fine pass time, as well as a great career that any Lumberjane could find herself enjoying. It is the tendency for a Lumberjane to want to learn everything there is to know about the world at large. She will want

to learn, and she will want to discover and explore all the places that haven't yet been touched by civilization. There are so many amazing worlds out there and this camp is only the beginning. There are many exercises the Lumberjanes will find at this camp that will help them find the tools and training they need to make all of this possible for them.

To obtain the *Snow-Globe Trotter* badge, a Lumberjane must keep a journal of her discoveries as she travels through the camp. With the help of her cabin, she will connect with the nature around her and create a map of the area. She will gain basic survival skills of what to do in the wilderness, and she will learn the amazing art of mapmaking. She will be able to be identify plants from all over the globe, as well as know the traits of poisonous plants, so that she should come across something unknown she will be able to ensure that none of her

will co...

The u...
It he...
appearan...
dress f...
Further...
Lumber...
to have...
part in...
Thiskv...
Hardc...
have...
them...

...out grows her uniform or ...ter Lumberjane.

I JUST CAN'T TENT TODAY, GUYS...

ROSIE IS SO NOT AMOOSED

The...
yellow, short sl...
emb...
the w...
choose...
slacks,...
made o...
out-of-do...
green bere...
the colla...
Shoes ma...
heels, roun...
socks shoul...
the uniform. Ne...es, bracelets, o...
belong with a Lumberjane unifor...

HOW TO WEAR...

To look well in a uniform ...
uniform be kept in good co...
pressed. See that the skirt is the rig...
height and build, that the belt is adjus...
that your shoes and stockings are in keeping with the
uniform, that you watch your posture and carry yourself
with dignity and grace. If the beret is removed indoors,
be sure that your hair is neat and kept in place with an
insconspicuous clip or ribbon. When you wear a
Lumberjane uniform you are identified as a member of
this organization and you should be doubly careful to
conduct yourself in a way that will show everyone that
courtesy and thoughtfullness are part of being a
Lumberjane. People are likely to judge a whole nation by
the selfishness of a few individuals, to criticize a whole
family because of the misconduct of one member, and to
feel unkindly toward and organization because of the

The unifor...
helps to cre...
in a group...
active life th...
another bond...
future, and pr...
in order to b...
Lumberjane pr...
Penniquiqul Thi...
Types, but m...
can either b... uniform, or make it themselves from
materials available at the trading post.

THIS STORM IS SNOW JOKE!

LUMBERJANES FIELD MANUAL
CHAPTER FOURTEEN

Lumberjanes "Literature" Program Field

THE MYSTERY OF HISTORY BADGE

"It's not about what's remembered, it's about why."

The amazing thing about memory is that it can be tricked. You can go through life knowing one thing as a fact but still be proven wrong at a later date. This is because if someone believes in something strong enough, they can make it feel like a fact for them. They can make something the truth, even though it wasn't. Which is why history is important, but might not always be reliable. As a Lumberjane, it will be important to not only keep an open mind to the occurrences around you but to stay on top of all the changes that happen around you. Everyone has their own unique experience, even if it's all the same event, because we are all unique individuals with our own unique backgrounds. This is what makes us great, what makes us human, what makes us Lumberjanes. All Lumberjanes must have a journal that they keep on themselves and use these journals to keep track of the events that happen to them at this camp, and hopefully the events that happen outside of the camp as well.

The Mystery of History badge is a badge that can only be earned in the library. Every scout will go to the camp's library and pick out a book. It can be any book, from humor to non-fiction, and they will research everything that went into the creation of the book. They will learn about the authors, about their life, about what inspired them to create the book and find all the information that they wouldn't be able to find in the book they chose by itself. One of the many fun opportunities with this badge is the chance to get a better knowledge of how things change from what actually happened to what ends up on paper. Capture the flag will be and will always be the biggest battle of the summer, but the real challenge to the game actually isn't getting the flag. It's breaking out of your enemies prison.

To obtain *The Mystery of History* badge a Lumberjane

"...she's planning to bag her biggest kill yet."

will co...

The...

It he...
appearan...
dress fo...
Further...
Lumber...
to have...
part in...
Thiskw...
Hardc...
have...
them...

OH FOR THE LOVE OF NELLIE BLY!

THE COLD NEVER BOTHERED US ANYWAY...

...E UNIFORM

...hould be worn at camp
...vents when Lumberjanes
...n may also be worn at other
...ions. It should be worn as a
...the uniform dress with
...rrect shoes, and stocking or

...out grows her uniform or
...ter Lumberjane.
...a she has
...h her
...f her

The...
yellow, short sl...
emb...
the w...
choose...
slacks,...
made o...
out-of-do...
green bere...
the colla...
Shoes ma...
heels, rou...
socks sho...
the uniform. Ne... es, bracelets, or other jewelry do...
belong with a Lumberjane uniform.

...real explorer o...
...doors is just outside your door, whether
...l or a country dweller. Get acquainted
...to use all the ways of getting

HOW TO WEAR THE UNIFOR...

To look well in a uniform dema...
uniform be kept in good condit...
pressed. See that the skirt is the right...
height and build, that the belt is adjus...
that your shoes and stockings are in k...
uniform, that you watch your posture and...
with dignity and grace. If the beret is remo...
be sure that your hair is neat and kept in pla...
insconspicuous clip or ribbon. When you wear a
Lumberjane uniform you are identified as a member of
this organization and you should be doubly careful to
conduct yourself in a way that will show everyone that
courtesy and thoughtfullness are part of being a
Lumberjane. People are likely to judge a whole nation by
the selfishness of a few individuals, to criticize a whole
family because of the misconduct of one member, and to
feel unkindly toward and organization because of the

The unifor...
helps to cre...
in a group...
active life th...
another bond...
future, and pr...
in order to b...
Lumberjane pr...
Penniquiqul Thi...
Types, but m...
can either b...
materials available at the trading post.

A TRAPDOOR? TOTES UNCOOL, LADY

LUMBERJANES FIELD MANUAL
CHAPTER FIFTEEN

Lumberjanes "Cooking" Program Field

OUT OF THYME BADGE

"Sometimes expediency is necessary."

Timeliness is next to godliness, or so the saying goes. For a Lumberjane, timeliness is an essential part of everyday life. There are many things that a Lumberjane will learn while at camp, she will learn how to care for the wildlife around her and how to use it to better her life and those around her. She will learn the importance of social customs and manners while at the same time enjoying the chance to break the boundaries that society might place upon her. And above all else, a Lumberjane will learn the importance of being on time.

The *Out of Thyme* badge is not just another badge that helps a Lumberjane understand the importance of seasoning, but it is a badge that helps teach the importance of knowing what time it is and constantly using that to her advantage. Need to slow cook a beef brisket, carve additional chairs for your guests and feed the bees that your neighbor left in your care while

they went on their annual Everest hike? Understanding how to use time is the key solution to ensuring that a Lumberjane is not only able to get all of that done, but is able to do it with enough time to spare that they'll be able to handle anything else life might throw her way.

To obtain the *Out of Thyme* badge, a Lumberjanes must show her understanding of spices in the kitchen. On top of that, a Lumberjane must also prove her time management skills through various timed courses. On top of that, she will have to complete several balanced meals in which she will have to feed her cabin. If the cabin decides to earn this badge as a team, which is encouraged, then the cabin will be asked to serve a meal for the entire class. They will have to gather the ingredients themselves, and with the help of their counselor, they will use the kitchens. It is also important that the Lumberjane cleans up after themselves as they

will co...

The...
It hel...
appearan...
dress f...
Further...
Lumber...
to have...
part in...
Thiskv...
Hardc...
have...
them...

WE WERE READY TO KICK SNOW MUCH BUTT!

WE FOUND JEN!

...E UNIFORM

...should be worn at camp
...events when Lumberjanes
...m may also be worn at other
...ions. It should be worn as a
...the uniform dress with
...rrect shoes, and stocking or

...out grows her uniform or
...ter Lumberjane.
...a she has
...her
...her

The...
yellow, short sl...
emb...
the w...
choose...
slacks,...
made o...
out-of-dc...
green bere...
the colla...
Shoes ma...
heels, rou...ings or
socks shou...ith the shoes or wi...
the uniform. Ne...ces, bracelets, or other jewelry do...
belong with a Lumberjane uniform.

THYME

HOW TO WEAR THE UNIFOR...

To look well in a uniform demans fir...
uniform be kept in good conditio...
pressed. See that the skirt is the right...
height and build, that the belt is adjusted...
that your shoes and stockings are in keeping...
uniform, that you watch your posture and carry you...
with dignity and grace. If the beret is removed indoors,...
be sure that your hair is neat and kept in place with an
insconspicuous clip or ribbon. When you wear a
Lumberjane uniform you are identified as a member of
this organization and you should be doubly careful to
conduct yourself in a way that will show everyone that
courtesy and thoughtfullness are part of being a
Lumberjane. People are likely to judge a whole nation by
the selfishness of a few individuals, to criticize a whole
family because of the misconduct of one member, and to
feel unkindly toward and organization because of the

e unifor...
elps to cre...
in a group...
active life th...
another bond...
future, and pr...
in order to b...
Lumberjane pr...
Penniquiqul Thi...
Types, but m...
can either b...
materials available at the trading post.

ABIGAIL HAS AN EXPLOSIVE PERSONALITY

LUMBERJANES FIELD MANUAL

CHAPTER SIXTEEN

Lumberjanes "Automotive" Program Field

SPARE ME BADGE

"Automobile safety saves."

Like any well rounded young woman, a Lumberjane will understand the importance of automobile safety. The key to this knowledge is understanding the vehicle inside and out. The Lumberjanes will be responsible for the care and upkeep of the camp vehicle in the summer that they are at the camp. The counselor in charge of the auto shop will educate each Lumberjane on how to identify parts of the engine, understand the common problems that are faced on the road, as well as the way to solve those problems with the tools available to them.

Life on the open road will be an experience that most will go through as they transition through their life, and even if it's an experience that not everyone will enjoy, it's definitely something a Lumberjane should be prepared for. From safety features like seat belts to how to change a tire, the *Spare Me* badge is about understanding practical knowledge of automobiles. As a Lumberjane,

our campers will understand the importance of keeping their property in tip top shape. They will have experience in taking care of their own belongings as well as helping others with their own, and they will be able see the benefit of taking the time to ensure their property is in great quality so that it will last for a long time.

To obtain the *Spare Me* badge a Lumberjane must choose the camp vehicle they will want to work on. They will learn all practical knowledge there is about the vehicle and will learn safety guidelines and laws from their home state. They will change the oil in the car, and they will learn how to change a flat tire. If they are of age, they will learn how to drive the vehicle without supervision and will be used to help transport campers or run other errands that might be needed. They will meet with the park ranger to talk about the dangers of driving in the mountains, what to look out for if off

will co

The u
It help
appearan
dress fe
Further
Lumber
to have
part in
Thiskw
Hardc
have e
them

**MO MONEY,
MO PROBLEMS...**

**FOR ONCE, JEN
DROVE US CRAZY!**

The
yellow, short sl
emb
the w
choose
slacks,
made o
out-of-do
green bere
the colla
Shoes ma
heels, rou   ngs on
socks should   th the shoes or wit
the uniform. Ne   es, bracelets, or other jewelry do
belong with a Lumberjane uniform.

HE UNIFORM

should be worn at camp
events when Lumberjanes
may also be worn at other
ions. It should be worn as a
the uniform dress with
rrect shoes, and stocking or
out grows her uniform or
ster Lumberjane.
a she has
her
her

HOW TO WEAR

To look well in a uniform
uniform be kept in goo
pressed. See that the skirt i
height and build, that the b
that your shoes and stocking
uniform, that you watch your post
with dignity and grace. If the beret is removed indoors,
be sure that your hair is neat and kept in place with an
insconspicuous clip or ribbon. When you wear a
Lumberjane uniform you are identified as a member of
this organization and you should be doubly careful to
conduct yourself in a way that will show everyone that
courtesy and thoughtfullness are part of being a
Lumberjane. People are likely to judge a whole nation by
the selfishness of a few individuals, to criticize a whole
family because of the misconduct of one member, and to
feel unkindly toward and organization because of the

TEAMWORK TO THE MAX!

The unifor
helps to cre
in a group.
active life th
another bond
future, and pr
in order to b
Lumberjane pr
Penniquiqul Thi   re Lady
Types, but m   es will wish to have one. They
can either b   the uniform, or make it themselves from
materials available at the trading post.

COVER GALLERY

Lumberjanes "Wildlife" Program Field

BADGER OF HONOR BADGE

"The more the merrier."

A Lumberjanes success is not based solely on the badges that she earns, but it can be a lot of fun to collect them all. There are hundreds of badges that a Lumberjane is able to earn, from the *Pungeon Master* badge to the beloved *Dye Hard* badge, in which Lumberjanes learn how to create dye from nature around them. In our Lumberjanes camp, we want all the Lumberjanes to only take on the badges that they are able to fit into their time at the camp, and if that means someone is able to tackle the whole handbook and it's several other volumes, then we applaud this individual. It is up to the camper to find every counselor, every possible teacher, to find out what badges she can earn in the time frame she has allotted.

If a Lumberjane scout is able to collect all the badges available to them at the time that this badge becomes available, then they will get the *Badger of Honor* badge, as well as a lesson in how to extend her sash in a tasteful

fashion. Though if they are already earning this badge then there is a good chance they they've already decides to extend their sash several times over. To the Lumberjane who decided to take on this challenge, keep in mind that competition is encouraged, as long as it remains happy, healthy, and non-detrimental to anyone else at the camp. The *Badger of Honor* badge is a badge earned because Lumberjanes never quit. Lumberjanes want to excel at everything they have the chance to. This is a badge earned by those who know what they want to accomplish and will be able to take on the challenge while most likely bringing their friends along for the ride.

To obtain the *Badger of Honor* badge, a Lumberjane must be persistent, she must keep her head up and tackle every obstacle that is thrown at her. She will go out of her way to find more badges for her to earn, and with the help of her friends, accomplish every task she sets forth

Issue Fifteen
BROOKE ALLEN WITH COLORS BY MAARTA LAIHO

Issue Fifteen Variant
RICARDO BESSA

Issue Fifteen ComiXology Exclusive
HOPE LARSON WITH COLORS BY MAARTA LAIHO

Issue Sixteen
BROOKE ALLEN WITH COLORS BY MAARTA LAIHO

Issue Sixteen Variant
KAT PHILBIN

Issue Seventeen Variant
JEN WANG